The Case of the
Furtive Firebug

The Case of the
Furtive Firebug

by
Peggy Nicholson
and John F. Warner

Lerner Publications Company / Minneapolis

Cover art by Christopher Nick

Library of Congress Cataloging-in-Publication Data

Nicholson, Peggy.
    The case of the furtive firebug / by Peggy Nicholson and
John F. Warner.
        p.   cm. —(Kerry Hill Casecrackers ; #1)
    Summary: Hally Watkins, her younger brother Jason, and
other young people they meet in Newport, Rhode Island, must
prove that their friend Tuyet is not responsible for burning
down the house she has been hired to paint.
    ISBN 0-8225-0709-9 :
    [1. Mystery and detective stories. 2. Arson—Fiction.]
I. Warner, J. F. (John F.) II. Title. III. Series: Nicholson, Peggy.
Kerry Hill Casecrackers ; #1.
PZ7.N5545Cam 1995
[Fic]—dc20   94-9200
                                                          CIP
                                                           AC

Manufactured in the United States of America
1 2 3 4 5 6 — I/BP — 00 99 98 97 96 95

To Jack, my mentor and friend,
with much affection.—P.N.

CONTENTS

1 Squids and Trouble   9

2 The Accidental Firebug   21

3 Maybe Werewolves Like Brown Paint   35

4 Where There's Smoke...   49

5 Trapped in the Dark   63

6 Accused!   75

7 Searching for Clues   88

8 The Kerry Hill Casecrackers   99

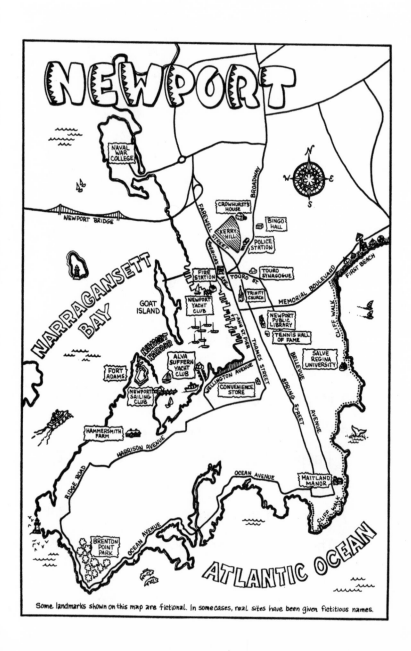

Some landmarks shown on this map are fictional. In some cases, real sites have been given fictitious names.

SQUIDS AND TROUBLE

For a little guy, Jason moved very fast. As he stalked up the sidewalk of the causeway to Goat Island, he didn't look back. "You don't even know her!" he growled. "Why are you giving her a birthday present?"

"Because I want to," Hally called after him. "She's my mother, too, you know."

Her little brother swung around on his heels and scowled at her. "You never gave her anything before," he said.

"Did so! Only you were too young to remember. Then, after you and Mom moved to Germany, I . . . I just never got around to it." Hally stopped suddenly and stared out over the low railing. Newport Harbor was blue today—as rich a blue as the sky above. Tiny cat's-paws of wind raked the surface of the water, and all the boats on their moorings swung to face them.

Jason walked back and stood beside Hally. He had to stand on tiptoe to see over the railing. "I'm not giving her anything," he muttered.

Hally looked down at the top of his brown head. His hair was the same color as their father's, and he had that same funny stick-up cowlick, just like Dad's. It was the first thing she'd noticed last night, when Jason got off the plane. That and how much he'd grown in the three years since she last saw him.

"You're just mad 'cause she sent you away for the summer," she said, then wished she hadn't.

Jason turned away from the water and trotted partway up the bridge ahead of her, his hands jammed into the pockets of his shorts.

"Hey, Jason, wait up!" she yelled, but he

dodged around an old woman who was fishing at the railing and kept going. Hally sucked in her breath as the next person along the railing swung back his pole, getting ready to cast. But Jason was short. The sharp hook swung over his head, then whipped forward and spun down and out into the water. Jason stopped to watch, and Hally caught up with him.

"Jason, you've got to watch out!" she scolded him.

"No, that's your job." Jason smirked at her and turned back to the fisherman.

And it looks like watching Jason is going to be the hardest job Dad ever gave me, Hally thought gloomily. Jason was too smart for his own good, and he was too mad to stay out of trouble.

"Why are you jerking your fishing pole like that?" Jason asked the fisherman.

"Jigging for squid," the man said, and jerked the pole again. "You snag 'em with a hook."

"Squid, wow!" Jason quickly slipped out of

Hally's grasp. He scampered up the sidewalk to where a dark-haired girl was fishing. She was jerking her fishing pole too, and when Hally looked beyond her, she could see fishing poles waving and twitching and jerking all the way along the causeway. Everybody was jigging for squid.

Jason almost dived headfirst into the tall white bucket that stood beside the girl. "Hally!" he shrieked. "Come look! Quick!" He reached into the bucket.

The girl jerked around as though someone had jigged *her*. "Hey! You cut that out!"

"Ugh!" Jason yelped, and drew back from the bucket so fast that he fell backward onto the sidewalk. "Ick!" From his sitting position, he shook out his hands. "Oh, yuk!" They were dripping with black ink.

The girl, who looked about Hally's age, laughed. She looked at Hally as if to share the joke. "Pick up a squid and you're going to get squirted," she told Jason. "Don't you know that?"

Hally moved carefully around Jason's flapping hands and looked in the bucket. It was filled with squid—brown ones and all kinds of flashy rainbow-colored ones. Their eyes were enormous. "He doesn't know about squid. He's from Iowa." A squid waved its legs at Hally, which gave her a funny feeling in the pit of her stomach. "I'm from Texas. I don't know anything about squid, either," she admitted.

"What are you doing in Rhode Island then?" the girl asked. She pulled a rag out of her box of fishing tackle and handed it to Jason.

"I came here with my dad," Hally explained, "and my brother is visiting us for the summer. Dad teaches high school in Texas, but he used to live here when he was in the navy. He found a job here for the summer, teaching kids how to sail at the Newport Sailing Club."

"Never heard of it." The girl picked up the

fishing rod she had propped against the railing and started reeling in her line.

Hally had never heard of the sailing club either, until her dad came up with his crazy idea to teach sailing. She wished she still didn't know about it. She'd rather be back home in Houston, helping her best friend, Lisa, exercise her horses. She didn't know anybody in Newport, and she hadn't met anyone her own age, even though she had been here almost a week.

Jason finished wiping squid ink off his hands, then bounced to his feet. "What are you gonna do with all those squid?" he asked.

"I sell them to my uncle. To cook in the restaurant where he works. He gives me a quarter for each one." The girl finished reeling in her line and set the pole aside.

"A quarter! That's a bargain!" Jason's hand dived into his pocket. "I'll give you a quarter for a squid."

"Sure," the girl laughed. "What will you do

with it, take it home in your pocket?" She knelt down and packed up her tackle box.

"I could do all kinds of neat things with a squid," Jason said.

Hally hated to imagine what. "What do they taste like?" she asked. She and the girl were leaning with their arms propped on the railing now, half watching each other and half watching a motor launch full of people approaching the causeway.

The girl wrinkled her nose as she considered the question. "Ohhh . . . sort of like a french fry, or sort of like a rubber band. Depends on how long you cook 'em."

They laughed, then Hally said, "My name's Hally. Hally Watkins. Actually, it's Harriet Lee, but I like Hally a lot better. I'm almost thirteen, and my brother Jason just turned eight." She tipped her head in the direction of Jason, who'd been standing over the squid bucket muttering to himself the last time she looked.

The girl smiled shyly. "I'm Tuyet—Nguyen Tuyet. I'm twelve."

Glad to meet you, Hally thought—*awfully glad.* She nodded at the motor launch that was about to pass under them. "Where are they going?"

"That's the harbor launch. It takes people out to their boats on the other side of the causeway." As Tuyet turned to point out the boats floating at their moorings, she gasped. "Your brother!"

Jason was hanging over the railing, holding Tuyet's fishing rod and dangling its line toward the launch. If he leaned out any farther, he would topple right into the boat twenty feet below! Hally started for him, then froze. If she startled him, he'd tip over the railing for sure.

"*Hey!*" yelled a man from below.

Hally looked to see who was yelling. A man in the launch was scowling and trying to grab something dancing in the air in front of him—a squid. The squid's arms flopped up and down—

it was dangling from Jason's fishing line! Eyeball to eyeball with the creature, the man swore aloud. He slashed at the squid with a long fishing knife.

But Jason jerked his pole up and down, keeping the squid just out of the man's reach.

"Jason!" Hally howled.

Jason cackled as he jerked the squid straight up over the man's head. The launch continued on under the causeway and out of sight. Hally grabbed her brother and yanked—hard. He collapsed at her feet, laughing too hard to stand up. Tuyet snatched her pole back and began reeling in the squid. "Jason, I can't believe—"

"Did you *see?*" Jason waved his feet in the air and hugged himself with glee. "Did you?"

"Hey, you up there!" It was the same angry voice roaring up from below. Hally peeked carefully over the railing. The launch had spun around and come back under the causeway. Now it floated below, its engine idling.

The man Jason had teased wore the angriest face Hally had ever seen. His black mustache bristled. "If you weren't up there, and me down here, I'd...I'd...I'd..." He was too mad to say what he'd do. With his red face, he looked like a cherry bomb about to explode.

"Me?" Hally squeaked. "It wasn't—"

But he couldn't hear her over the sound of the engine. He shook his big knife at her. Then he growled something at the launch driver, who backed the boat away from the causeway and headed off toward the moorings. Several people in the launch were glaring up at her and muttering angrily. Hally was glad she couldn't hear what they were saying.

Her knees gave out and she dropped out of their sight, behind the railing. She nearly landed on Tuyet, who was cowering beside her, her eyes as big as a scared squid's. Jason still lay flat on his back, laughing and pointing at the two of them.

"Oh, no," Tuyet moaned. "That was Mr. Crowhurst! I hope he didn't see me."

"Who's Mr. Crowhurst?" Hally wanted to know.

"Just the meanest, cheapest man in Newport, if not all Rhode Island," Tuyet answered. "I'm supposed to do some painting in one of his houses. But if he saw me, I'll be fired before I get started."

Hearing this, Jason rolled over onto his side and stopped giggling. "If this guy is such a jerk, why do you want to work for him?"

Tuyet looked at Jason. "Because getting a job when you're twelve years old isn't easy. And I want the money."

"Well," Jason said, "all I can say is, if you work for this Crowhurst guy, you're as much of a jerk as he is."

"Jason!" Hally hissed. "You apologize to Tuyet, right now!"

Instead, Jason pulled himself to his feet with

a scornful grunt. "I'm going home," he said, heading down the sidewalk.

The two girls looked at each other and shook their heads. "I'm glad he's your brother and not mine," Tuyet said.

Hally made a face. If today was any indication, it was going to be a long, long summer.

CHAPTER 2

THE ACCIDENTAL FIREBUG

The kitchen floor was almost pretty, with red splashes of spaghetti sauce decorating it. Hally squatted by the biggest pool and started wiping with a paper towel. Nearby, Jason was using his hands to scoop up the sauce and pour it back into the pot. He looked so miserable, she almost wanted to smile. It was hard to stay angry at Jason. "You're a big help," she told him.

"Yeah, a big help," he muttered. "Any time you want your supper spilled..." He stopped scooping and glared at his red hands.

What was she going to feed them all for supper, Hally wondered, now that Jason had knocked the sauce off the stove? Back home in Texas, she and her dad took turns cooking. But since they'd been in Newport, Hally had done most of it. Teaching sailing and working a second job with a caterer had kept her dad very busy.

But that was okay, Hally liked to cook. Spaghetti was one of their favorite meals—but not after the sauce had sloshed around the kitchen floor. Tuna melts would have to do for tonight's meal.

To distract Jason, she went back to what they'd been talking about before the disaster. "If I had a fishing pole like Tuyet's, I could catch squids to sell. It'd be nice to make some money of my own, so I wouldn't have to ask Dad all the time."

"*If* you had a fishing pole," Jason said. "Mom always says, 'If we had some ham, we could have ham and eggs, if we had some eggs.'"

Hally laughed. "Dad says that, too! What else does she say?"

Jason made a red handprint on the floor,

then frowned down at it. "She says, 'Turn off your light, Jase, it's after 10:00. That book'll be there in the morning.'" He drew a face in the red sauce below his handprint, turning it into a goofy-looking moose. "Or she says, 'I don't care if you did wash this morning. Go wash your hands and face again.'" Jason's eyes were suddenly shiny. "Just stupid mom stuff, that's all. I hate—" He swiped his hand across the floor, smearing his doodle.

Hally wanted to hug him, but she thought she'd better not. "You can't hate her," she said. "She's your . . . our . . . mother."

Jason started scooping up sauce again. "I don't hate her. It's the Hyena I hate. I think he made her send me away."

This was news to Hally. Dad said Jason was visiting because they hadn't seen him in so long.

After Hally and Jason's parents divorced, they had all continued living in Houston, with Hally and Jason living one month at their mother's

condominium and the next month at their
father's townhouse. But then their mother was
offered a job teaching school on an American
army base in Germany. She had wanted to take
Hally and Jason with her. Hally's father didn't
like the idea at all, and Hally had balked at leaving her friends in Houston.

On the other hand, Jason had thought it
would be fun to live in another country, and he
had always been especially close to their mother.
So he'd gone with her to Germany. The two had
returned to the United States less than six
months ago. This time they settled in Iowa,
where their mother had taken a job at a small
college.

"Who's the Hyena?" Hally asked.

Jason told her while she finished wiping up
the sauce. The Hyena was Hiram Abrams, a pro-
fessor at the college where their mother taught.
He had freckles—lots of them—and red hair.

"And he laughs all the time," Jason growled.

"Like this—Hoo *hoo*, haw *haw* haw *haw!* I hate him!"

They were interrupted by a knock on the back screen door. "Hello, anybody home?" Tuyet called.

"Hey!" Hally ran to let her in. She hadn't seen Tuyet since yesterday. She and Jason had helped Tuyet carry the squid home, and they had learned that Tuyet also lived on Kerry Hill, just one block from their house. "We stopped by this morning, but you weren't there. What's up, Tuyet?"

Tuyet looked around the big kitchen. "I was helping my uncle chop vegetables at the restaurant. On my way home, I met Mr. Crowhurst."

"Uh-oh!" Hally groaned. "Was he mad about the squid?"

Tuyet wrinkled her nose. "No...it's very funny, but he wasn't. Oh, he was grumpy, he always is. But he said he could take a joke as well as the next guy, then he asked me if I still wanted to paint an apartment for him. You said you'd like to make some money, so I wondered—"

"If I'd like to help?" Hally caught her new friend by the arm. "Tell me about it."

They walked out onto the deck, with Jason following them. The way Hally saw it, the deck was the best thing about the place. Their apartment was the top two floors of an old three-story house, and the deck was off the second floor. From the deck, she could see a small patch of the harbor through the trees, and she could also look down into the backyards of the Kerry Hill neighborhood. A set of outside stairs led down to their backyard. She and Tuyet stayed on the deck and sat on the picnic table.

"So what's this painting job all about?" Hally asked.

"Mr. Crowhurst owns a lot of rental apartments around town. He asked if I could paint a couple of rooms in one of them. Someone's going to be moving in the day after tomorrow, and he can't get a regular painter on such short notice."

"If he's half as grouchy as he was yesterday, no wonder," Hally said.

"Oh, he is," Tuyet said. "I can barely stand him, but I need the money."

"Why?" Jason asked.

"I'm saving up to help Uncle Chau-Li buy the restaurant he works in," Tuyet said.

Jason looked stubborn. "But if you really don't like the guy—"

Hally cut Jason off. "Why *do* you dislike him so much? Just because he's a grouch?"

Tuyet shrugged. "It's more than that. He teases me, and not in a very funny way, though he smiles when he says it. He calls me a crazy foreign firebug!"

Hally remembered the look on Crowhurst's face in the launch. It was hard to picture him smiling. "Why does he call you that, a firebug?"

Tuyet smiled. "That's a long story." But she

made it a good one. "Last winter, I was helping my uncle clear tables at the restaurant. Someone had left a pack of cigarettes on a table, so I took it home. I always wondered what they taste like."

"How do they taste?" Jason asked eagerly.

"Like burned broccoli, only worse! It was so bad I felt sick. I threw the cigarette into the wastebasket in my room and ran to the bathroom. After I threw up, I brushed my teeth and washed my face. Next thing I knew, Aunt Lam was yelling 'Fire! Fire!' Uncle Chau-Li was splashing buckets of water everywhere around my bedroom, and then the fire trucks came!

"The firefighters put out the fire quickly enough, but some of my wallpaper was ruined. All the neighbors came out to see what the trouble was! And then the next day the newspaper printed a story about it. They called it 'Youthful Escapade Ends in Near Disaster!'" Tuyet rolled her eyes.

"Wow," Hally said. "That must have been

awful! Did your aunt and uncle punish you?"

Tuyet shook her head. "Uncle Chau-Li said I'd taught myself my own lesson. But I had to strip all the wallpaper off the walls in my bedroom, and then paint it. That was a lot of work." She paused a moment, then went on. "But now everybody has forgotten all about it, except for Mr. Crowhurst. He keeps teasing me. You'd think he'd know how awful fires are. One of his rental houses burned to the ground last year!"

"Really? How?" Hally asked.

Tuyet shrugged. "The house was very old. They said it must have been the electrical wires, or maybe the furnace."

"So," Jason demanded, "if Crowhurst is a teaser and a grouch, how come your uncle and aunt let you work for him?"

Hally punched her brother on the arm, but Tuyet didn't seem to mind the question. "At first they didn't want me to," she admitted. "But I talked them into it. 'What can happen?'

I said. Then today I told them I would bring you along."

"Well," Hally laughed. "In that case, we have to come with you, to make sure you're okay."

So that was how, after supper, Hally and Jason came to be walking through a dense fog along a dead-end street that ran past an old graveyard. It was the type of night that sometimes gave Hally the creeps. "Do you think there are were-wolves out there?" Jason asked, sounding as if he almost hoped there were.

"No," Hally said firmly. She had enough trouble without werewolves. Her arms were full of paint buckets, a stack of old newspapers, a couple of paintbrushes, and two paint rollers that she had borrowed from their landlords, Mr. and Mrs. Ames, who lived downstairs. And she'd had lots of trouble persuading Dad to let her help Tuyet.

"Why do you have to paint this apartment so late in the day?" he'd asked.

Talking very fast, Hally had explained that Mr. Crowhurst's new tenants were supposed to move in very soon, so he needed it painted right away. That might mean they'd walk home after dark, she'd had to admit. But the house was only about three blocks away. And if she needed help of any sort, she'd run and ask the Ameses, since her dad would be working late, teaching an evening course on boat navigation.

"Which house is it?" Jason asked. He had his own arms full of another stack of newspapers and a jar of paste. Hally had told him he absolutely could not help paint, but he hadn't minded. He had something else to do, he had said mysteriously.

"That's it over there," Hally said, nodding at the very last house on the block. The house looked as spooky as the street. The paint was peeling off its clapboards, and its front porch sagged. One window on the second floor was broken. With a piece of cardboard nailed over the empty pane, the house looked like a giant, crouching ogre with one blind eye. Hally was happy to see Tuyet waving to them from the front steps.

"Now all we need is Mr. Crowhurst," Tuyet said. "He's supposed to meet me here and show me where to paint. That's his van there." She pointed to a battered blue van that was parked in front of the house. "I knocked on the door, but nobody answered."

Just then, the door behind Tuyet swung slowly, silently open. A very tall man loomed in the doorway and looked down at them. He had a bushy black mustache that curled down over his lips, and a mouth that didn't smile. His grease-stained jeans had holes in both knees. "What are they doing here?" Mr. Crowhurst growled at Tuyet.

"These are my friends," Tuyet said. "They're going to help me paint." She touched Hally's arm. "This is—"

"I know who she is!" Mr. Crowhurst broke in, glaring at Hally. "She's the brat on the causeway. The one who tried to drop a squid on my head."

"I didn't—" Hally protested.

But Mr. Crowhurst wasn't listening. He jabbed his finger at Tuyet. "I hired you, not a whole circus of kids! I don't want any paint splashed around, and you'll do a better job if you work alone. Too many cooks spoil the soup."

"That's broth," Jason spoke up. "Too many cooks spoil the *broth*."

"We're really very neat, Mr. Crowhurst," Hally said quickly, but it was too late. Jason had spoiled everything.

Mr. Crowhurst was too busy glaring at Jason to even look at her. "*You* are the one who's going to be in the *stew*, midget, if you don't get out of here," he roared. "Now, get!"

And so they "got." Hally wanted to tell Tuyet to come with them and not to work for such a horrible man. But Tuyet cut her off with a tiny shake of her head. She plainly meant to complete the job, even if Mr. Crowhurst was a mean-tempered grouch.

The last time Hally and Jason looked back, Tuyet was following Crowhurst through the dark doorway. The fog seemed to envelop the one-eyed house. As Hally and Jason walked away, the house and the blue van parked in front of it—the whole end of the street—faded and finally vanished in the mist.

CHAPTER 3

MAYBE WEREWOLVES LIKE BROWN PAINT

"And you said there were no werewolves around here," Jason muttered as they looked back at the fog.

Hally shivered. She knew what he meant. It wasn't just all that hair on Crowhurst's face. He had mean eyes. "I've got to go back," she said. "I can't let Tuyet work alone in that creepy old house."

"Then let's go!" Jason turned and headed back down the street.

It was no use telling him to go home and wait for her there, Hally knew. She shrugged and hurried after him. "I bet Crowhurst is too cheap to pay two painters," she said. "That's why he sent us away. So I'll just help Tuyet paint for free. He can't complain about that."

But Mr. Crowhurst had looked like he would complain about anything, so when they reached the house again, Hally and Jason tiptoed up the stairs to the porch. The front door was unlocked, and Hally held her breath as they pushed it open. The hinges didn't creak. Somehow that seemed even spookier than if they had.

Inside, a single dim, unshaded lightbulb stared down from the ceiling like a yellow eyeball. It barely lit the big, dusty hallway. There was a door to the right, which Hally figured would lead to the first-floor apartment. A stairway led up into the shadows.

Moving in slow motion, Jason turned the doorknob of the apartment door while Hally watched. "It's locked," he whispered.

Hally pointed at the ceiling to let Jason know she wanted to go to the second-floor apartment.

He nodded. Side by side, they crept up the stairs. When one of the steps squeaked loudly, they froze in place. But Crowhurst didn't come running and roaring.

As they reached the top step, Hally heard the man's grumbling voice. It came from a door that stood open a few inches. A line of light spilled out of the apartment, showing her another door across the hall. Towing Jason by his shirtsleeve, Hally slipped past the open door. She tried the door across from it. When it opened, they were looking into a broom closet. "Inside," she whispered.

With the closet door open a crack, they could peek out at the apartment door. Crowhurst's voice grew louder, as if he were moving closer to them. "What do you mean, you can't smell any cats?" he asked. "My last renters had eight cats in here. That's why I want this room and the kitchen painted—to freshen the place up. The new renters are moving in the day after tomorrow. So you'd better do a nice, neat job, see?"

"I wouldn't rent an apartment from that werewolf if he were the last—mmph!" Jason finished, as Hally clamped a hand over his mouth.

"I will," Tuyet's voice came faintly from across the hall.

"Okay, then," Crowhurst said. "You've got everything you need. I'm going over to the bingo hall. But I'll be back to check on you when the games are over. I want you here waiting for me. Don't go home, even if you finish tonight. I want to make sure your work's worth paying for."

"Oh, it will be," Tuyet promised. She sounded very polite, and very, very angry.

"Here, give me your sneakers," Crowhurst said.

"My shoes?"

"Yeah, give 'em here. If you step in any paint, I don't want you tracking it around on the floor. If you paint barefoot, you can't say you didn't know you stepped in it. I'll put them outside on the porch for you." Crowhurst passed in front of the door again. Then Hally and Jason jumped as rock music suddenly blared out into the hallway.

Crowhurst had to shout to be heard above the music. "Thought you'd like a radio to keep you company. So get hopping. I'll be back in a few hours." The apartment door suddenly opened wide, and the light that poured from the room cast Crowhurst's shadow on the hallway floor. He shut the door behind him, and the radio wasn't quite so loud.

Peeking through the crack in the closet door, Hally felt the hair on her neck rise. Crowhurst seemed to be looking right at them!

Then he turned away, and she let her breath out again. He went down the stairs, carrying Tuyet's shoes.

"Whew!" Jason exclaimed, and he started to push the door open.

Hally held him back. "Wait till we're sure he's gone."

So Jason chanted under his breath, "One potato, two potato, three potato, four. Five potato, six potato, lemme open the door!"

The house shook as Crowhurst slammed the front door below, and Hally let Jason go. "Quiet now."

"He couldn't hear us over that music if we screamed," Jason said and pushed out into the hall.

Tuyet nearly did scream when they walked into the apartment. She was standing with her back to the door, studying the room. She turned and jumped a foot.

Hally walked over to the radio, turned it down, and smiled at Tuyet. "We thought you might like some company," she said, "so we snuck back."

Tuyet's face showed her relief. "You thought right! I think that man is crazy!"

"This place doesn't smell like cats," Jason

said. He sniffed as hard as he could, his eyes growing big as he sucked in the air.

"That's what I mean," Tuyet said. "And look at the walls. Do they look like they need painting?"

They didn't. The walls were old rough plaster, but the white paint on them looked pretty fresh to Hally. "Maybe he's got a better nose than we do."

"Nobody's got a better nose than me," Jason bragged. But they couldn't think of any other explanation that made sense. So Tuyet and Hally shrugged their shoulders and went to work.

Crowhurst hadn't given Tuyet a drop cloth to protect the floor while she painted, so Hally took some of the newspapers she'd brought along and spread them out on the floor by the walls. Jason spread out his own papers and sat on the floor near the radio. He hummed along with the songs in a funny off-key voice that reminded Hally of their father.

41

"Ugh!" Tuyet exclaimed. She stared down into the can of paint she had opened. "Look at the color he wants to use. He *is* crazy!"

The new paint was an ugly shade of gray, and there wasn't much of it. Tuyet and Hally stared at each other, then they opened the other can. This can held a shade of brown that looked like mud.

"Maybe werewolves like those colors," Jason said when they showed him. He had set out a sheet of blank white paper on the floor in front of him, with his jar of paste beside it. He pulled a pair of scissors from his shirt pocket and started cutting up a newspaper.

"Whatever Mr. Crowhurst wants, Mr. Crowhurst gets," Tuyet said grimly. "But it will look awful, no matter how neat we are."

They decided to paint the living room brown and the kitchen gray. Hally lent Tuyet one of the Ameses' paint rollers, because the one Crowhurst had given her was nearly useless. It was stiff with old paint. They both covered their rollers with paint, then paused, staring at each other—did they really dare to do this? Then they laughed.

"One!" said Tuyet.

"Two!" Hally chanted, raising her roller.

"*Three!*" they cried and rolled the gloomy paint out onto the wall at the same time. They both groaned aloud at how awful it looked, and then giggled.

"Reminds me of making mud pies," Hally said.

"What's a mud pie?" Tuyet asked, so Hally told her while they worked.

Then, Tuyet told her about some of the counting games she and the other children had played on the boat to pass the time.

"What boat?" Hally asked.

"The boat when I left my country, Vietnam. My mother sent me out with a friend of hers." Tuyet put down her paint roller.

"You mean after the war?" Hally asked.

"Oh, it was years after that. But my father

had worked for the Americans, and so after, they . . . had a hard time. Then my father died when I was seven. That was when my mother decided there would be no life for me in Vietnam. My mother's friend brought me to America, to live with Aunt Lam and Uncle Chau-Li."

"But what about your mother?" Hally asked, then wished she hadn't.

Eyes shining, Tuyet turned away. She picked up her paint roller and attacked the wall with swift strokes. "I . . . I don't know," she murmured, so low that Hally could barely hear her.

They didn't speak again for a long while. Hally was sorry she had asked about Tuyet's mother. She disliked seeing her new friend sad.

Finally Hally said, "Tell me about the restaurant your uncle wants to buy." Tuyet seemed glad to change the subject and began to cheer up as she talked about the restaurant.

Hally held the ladder for her while she painted above one window, then Tuyet held it for Hally while she painted over the other window. Soon they were finished with one wall. They stood back and stared at it, and laughed. "Awful!" Tuyet pronounced.

"I sure wouldn't live here," Hally agreed.

"Would you mind moving?" Jason asked, kneeling at his sister's feet. "You're standing on a V."

Hally looked down. She was standing on the sports page of the *Newport Loudhailer*, the local daily newspaper. She lifted her foot. A headline blared: "PATRIOTS VICTORS AGAIN!"

"Perfect!" Jason gloated, as he slid the paper out from under her foot. Returning to his corner, he started cutting out the V.

"What are you making?" Tuyet asked. She walked over to Jason and looked at his white paper. Jason had cut out lots of letters of all shapes and sizes and colors from headlines and advertisements. Then he had pasted the letters down on the white paper to make words.

"I'm making an agronomist letter," Jason said without looking up. He caught his tongue between his teeth as he trimmed the inside of the V.

A little bell sounded in Hally's mind. "You mean an anonymous letter?" she asked.

"Yeah, I guess so," Jason smeared paste on the back of his V. "So he won't recognize my writing."

"He who?" Hally asked.

"The Hyena, who do you think?" Jason muttered. He pasted down the V with a smack of his fist. He glared at his paper for a moment, then picked up an *I* and began to spread paste on it.

"Who's the Hyena?" Tuyet wanted to know.

"Our mother's boyfriend," Hally explained, wondering what she could say to Jason to make him stop. "Our parents are divorced."

His letter said, "THE VIPER IS COMING IN..."

"What's a viper?" Tuyet asked.

Jason gave her an evil-looking grin. "Hoo *hoo,* haw *haw!*" he laughed in a big, fake hyena voice. "You don't know who the Viper is?"

"I think it's a snake," Hally said. "But Jason, you can't—"

"Oh, can't I?" He stood up. "I need a 2," he muttered to himself, looking around at the newspapers spread out on the floor. Then he lifted his head and sniffed the air.

"What is it?" Tuyet asked.

"I smell something." Jason sucked in so much air that his chest puffed out, making him look like a bullfrog.

"The cats?" Hally suggested, though she couldn't smell anything.

Jason shook his head and turned around, still sniffing.

"You're smelling the paint fumes," Tuyet told him.

Jason shook his head again and started for

the apartment door. "No, it's not that." He opened the door, stuck his head out into the hall and sniffed noisily. "It's smoke." He turned around and stared at them, and suddenly, with his eyes growing large, he didn't look like the worst nuisance Hally had ever met in her life. He looked like a small, scared, eight-year-old boy. "I smell something burning!"

CHAPTER 4

WHERE THERE'S SMOKE...

Hally didn't believe Jason—she didn't want to believe him. "I can't smell anything," she said firmly, putting a hand on his shoulder. She sniffed the air in the hallway and shook her head. "Nothing but paint smell. And if you do smell something burning, it's probably just from the people in the first-floor apartment. Maybe they burned their supper."

Tuyet came to stand beside them. "Nobody lives downstairs," she said in a small, tight voice. "Mr. Crowhurst said the other renters moved out last month. There's nobody in this house but us."

Hally wished Tuyet hadn't said that. Her words sounded tiny and scared.

"I do smell smoke!" Jason whispered urgently.

Hally sniffed again. She could smell paint, as well as damp musty wood. Like most of the big, old houses in Newport, this one was built completely of wood. If there were a fire... She shivered. "Well," she whispered, then she said it again in a louder voice, a voice that sounded braver than she felt. "Well, if you think you smell smoke, Jason, I guess I'd better go check it out."

"We," said Tuyet. "*We* will check it out."

"You're not leaving me!" Jason scampered along beside her, staying close.

"Of course not," Hally said. "You're our champion nose. So let's just go down and have a smell around."

Sniffing loudly, they went down the stairs, with Hally and Jason in the lead. Tuyet followed so close behind that she kept stepping on Hally's heels with her bare feet.

At the bottom of the stairs, they stopped and inhaled deliberately. "It's getting stronger," Jason said.

Tuyet looked at Hally over his head and wrinkled her forehead. *Do you smell it?* that look said. Hally bit her lip and shook her head. But Jason looked so certain. Maybe he did have a champion nose.

"It's in here?" Hally asked him as they walked to the door of the first-floor apartment.

Jason nodded.

Hally tried the door. "It's locked, Jason." She turned the doorknob all the way clockwise, then all the way counterclockwise. The door wouldn't budge. "If there's nobody there, then how could a fire start?"

Jason didn't try to answer Hally. He knelt down and stuck his nose to the crack under the door. "I do smell smoke!" he insisted. "It smells like cigarettes."

Tuyet crouched down by Jason. "Then that's

the answer, Jason," she said in a patient voice. "I bet the last people who rented this place were smokers. You do have a super nose if you can still smell their old cigarettes."

Jason sat up and glared at her. "What do you think my nose is—stupid? This is new smoke, not old smoke."

Tuyet shrugged and looked up at Hally as if to ask, *What now?*

Hally shrugged back. "Well, there's not anything we can do about it, Jason," she said. "So I guess maybe we should keep on painting, and you can tell us if the smell gets any worse."

"Okay, you guys, *don't* believe me!" Jason bounced to his feet. "But don't ask me to smell for you. I wouldn't tell you if your pet poodle was on fire!" He pounded up the stairs and out of sight.

"Gosh, he sure gets mad fast," Tuyet said. Then she looked at Hally and giggled. "Do you have a poodle?"

Hally smiled and shook her head, but still, she felt bad for Jason. She didn't want to hurt his feelings. They turned toward the stairs, then froze as they both heard a sound.

"*Uh-Shhhush!*" The sound came from the locked apartment.

Tuyet's mouth slowly formed a big O.

"*Shhooo!*" It sounded like someone trying very hard not to sneeze.

Tuyet caught Hally's arm and squeezed. "Did you hear that?" she whispered.

Hally nodded. "Come *on!*" Side by side, they scampered up the stairs—trying to run and tip-toe all at the same time. At the top of the stairs they stopped to catch their breath and to listen. But nothing moved down in the dim hallway below.

"Could it have been the wind?" Hally asked under her breath.

"A ghost?" Tuyet suggested. "It's a very old house."

Hally didn't even want to think about that! "The pipes," she said, "or maybe a bat?"

"Ugh!" Tuyet dragged her toward the apartment door.

As they reached it, Hally dug in her heels to stop them both. "Wait, Tuyet, listen!"

Tuyet swung back and listened, her eyes dark and fearful.

"No, I mean listen to me," Hally said. "We can't tell Jason, okay? He's scared already."

Tuyet nodded. "And maybe we just imagined it?"

"I sure hope so!" And maybe they had, Hally thought as they entered the apartment. Nothing else made any sense at all.

Jason glanced up at them, then looked down at his letter again. His bottom lip stuck out and he was scowling. When he looked away, Hally turned the lock on the apartment door. Maybe they had imagined that sneeze, but she was taking no chances. Of course, if there were a ghost in this house, it could probably walk right through doors.

Tuyet was peeking over Jason's shoulder. He didn't look up as Hally came to see. His letter said, "THE VIPER IS COMING IN 2 MON ... "

"He's coming in two months?" Tuyet asked.

Jason shrugged but wouldn't answer.

So they went back to work. Hally turned the radio up even louder, and Tuyet's expression told her that she knew why. If there were a ghost out there someplace, they didn't want to hear it again.

The two girls were finishing the last mud-brown wall when Jason stood up and went over to the radio. He spun the dial, stopping when the sounds of a country-western band moaned its way into the room. "Oh, *yeah!*" he cried. "'Hurtin' for Certain' by the Broken Arrows. That's my favorite song!" He started shuffling his feet to the music, scuffing newspapers around the floor.

"Hey, you're good!" Tuyet laughed.

Jason ignored her as he shuffled into a weird, sliding, bobbing kind of dance step. It made Hally think of a duck trying to walk on greased Jell-O. She giggled. "That's great, Jason! What do you call that dance?"

"Oh, I'm hurtin' for certain," Jason sang and didn't reply. "Hurtin' for certain... Ever since you been flirtin'..."

"Come on, tell us," Hally coaxed. She went over beside him and tried to shuffle her feet the same way. "It's great. What's it called?"

"The Iowa Glide Stride," Jason sang, as he waddled away from her. "I invented it myself. Oh, I'm hurtin'—"

"*HEY!* Open up!" a man's voice roared.

Tuyet yelped and dropped her bucket of paint.

The door jumped in its frame as someone pounded on it. "Open up, Tuyet, you little fool!" the voice roared again.

"It's Mr. Crowhurst," Tuyet said.

Hally opened the door. Crowhurst burst into the room, and ran right past her. He stopped short as he saw Jason. "You!" he cried. "What are you doing here?"

"Oh, I'm hurtin' for certain," Jason sang and kept right on dancing. He bobbed and turned his back on the man.

"You'll be hurtin' for certain if you don't quit that fool dancing!" Crowhurst bellowed. "The house is on fire!" He caught Tuyet by the arm. "We have to get out of here!"

"I told you I smelled smoke!" Jason said.

Crowhurst shoved Hally toward the door. "Come on, you mouthy midget!" he yelled back at Jason. "Do you want to fry?"

For a second Hally thought Jason wasn't going to come at all. He scowled at Crowhurst, who was standing impatiently in the doorway. Then Jason snatched up his Viper letter and followed them into the hall.

As Crowhurst herded them down the stairs,

Hally could smell the smoke. It had a bitter, choking smell to it that made her cough. Crowhurst had let go of her to pick up Jason, who didn't look grateful—he looked mad enough to pop.

Tuyet and Hally reached the first floor together. The door to the apartment was now standing open. Smoke trickled out of the apartment and up to the ceiling.

Hally and Tuyet peered in the door. Inside the apartment, a lumpy, ragged old couch faced a black-and-white TV set. The TV was on, but the sound was turned off. A big ashtray rested on one arm of the couch, and a cigarette had slipped off the ashtray onto a cushion. Smoke rose around it and curled up to the ceiling.

"Hey, it's not too bad," Hally called over her shoulder. "We can put this out!" She started into the room. There was a window on either side of the couch, with long, ugly red curtains hanging down. The curtains draped over the couch at each end. If the fire got to those, then Mr. Crowhurst really would have a problem!

"Are you kidding?" The landlord caught Hally from behind and yanked her toward the door. "It's too dangerous! Get out of here!"

"My shoes!" Tuyet cried from the doorway. And looking back, Hally saw Tuyet's sneakers. They were propped against the footstool that sat in front of the couch—as if somebody had been wearing them while watching TV and then decided to be really comfortable, and kicked them off.

"Forget them!" Crowhurst yelled. Holding each of them by an elbow, he hustled them out of the apartment, out of the house, and down the steps to his van. Jason was already there.

Crowhurst opened the rear doors of his van. "Get in!" he hissed and pushed them inside. "We'll have to call the fire department!" he added. Jason came tumbling after them, and the doors slammed shut behind him. Crowhurst ran around to the front of the van. Hally couldn't see him; she could barely see anything. The front of the van was separated from the back by a metal wall, like Hally had seen in the van that her neighbor in Houston, a plumber, owned. Except the windows in Crowhurst's van were coated with paint. Hally heard the engine start with a roar, then they were racing wildly down the street.

"Ooof!" Jason grunted as they hit a bump. Hally and Tuyet clung to each other as the van careened around a corner. Then Crowhurst whipped around another corner, throwing Hally and Tuyet off balance. Something sharp was digging into Hally's back, but it was too dark to see what it was. It felt like a large screwdriver. She squirmed onto her stomach.

"Why doesn't he just stop at a house and call 911?" Tuyet wondered out loud.

"Maybe we're driving to the firehouse," Hally suggested. It seemed a stupid thing to do, but

Crowhurst was very upset. And she guessed she would be too, if it was her house that was burning down.

"I don't know where we are, we've turned so many times," Tuyet said, as the van finally screeched to a halt.

"I'm going to call the fire department!" Crowhurst called out as he climbed from the van. He slammed the door hard behind him. Then Hally, Tuyet, and Jason heard the sound of his footsteps running away.

"What do we do?" Tuyet asked. "Wait for him here?"

"No way!" Jason said. "I want to see the fire." He sat up and crawled over Hally to the back of the van. He rattled the door handle. "Hey, it's locked! He locked us in here!"

"He couldn't have!" Hally exclaimed. Scrambling back beside Jason, she grabbed the handle and tried to turn it. It wouldn't budge. Jason was right. They were locked in Crowhurst's van.

In the dark. And they didn't even know where they were.

"What if he forgets about us?" Jason asked.

Hally didn't have an answer to that one.

TRAPPED IN THE DARK

"He's not going to forget us," Tuyet said. "Once he calls the fire department, he'll come back."

"Right," Hally agreed. "We'll hear the fire trucks any minute now. Then I bet Mr. Crowhurst will drive us back to the house to watch them fight the fire."

That cheered up Jason for a few minutes. While they waited for Crowhurst to come back, Hally picked up the tools they were sitting on and stacked them out of the way in a corner of the van. Then she and Tuyet sat on either side of Jason. The three of them leaned against one wall of the van, shoulders touching.

Crowhurst must have parked near a street-light. A ray of light shone down through the van's skylight, casting a bright patch halfway up the other wall. Hally stared at the patch and listened for sirens.

"So where are the fire trucks?" Jason grumbled. He stirred and his elbow dug into Hally's ribs.

"Maybe we can't hear them from here," Hally said, but that seemed strange. Newport wasn't a big place. When the fire trucks were called out, you could hear their sirens from almost any part of town.

"And where's that dumb old Crowhurst?" Jason added. "He's been gone for hours!"

"It just seems that way," Hally assured him. But how long had Crowhurst been gone? Ten minutes? Fifteen? It shouldn't take that long to make a phone call. Maybe he'd walked back to the fire.

"You know what I'd like to know?" Tuyet said. "I'd like to know what my shoes were doing in that apartment."

"What are you talking about?" Jason asked. Crowhurst had pushed him out the front door so fast that he'd missed seeing Tuyet's sneakers.

So Hally and Tuyet told him what they'd seen in the first-floor apartment—the shoes, the smoldering cigarette, the television turned on.

"But the sound was turned all the way down?" Jason repeated. "That's weird!"

"Not as weird as my shoes," Tuyet said. "The door to that apartment was shut and locked, remember? So did my shoes walk in there by themselves?" She shivered.

"Maybe a ghost walked in wearing them." Jason giggled.

"That's not funny," Tuyet protested. "Ghosts are nothing to fool with."

"You really believe in ghosts?" Jason asked.

"Yes, I do. My uncle Chau-Li says . . . " Tuyet

shrugged, her shoulders rubbing against her friends. "Yes," she said stiffly, "I believe in them."

"Well, so do I," Jason admitted cheerfully. "But that doesn't mean I'm scared of them."

"Anyway, I've never heard of a ghost that smokes cigarettes," Hally said firmly. "And I'm sure if a ghost decided to watch TV, he'd turn on the sound like everyone else does."

"Maybe he switched it off 'cause a commercial was on," Jason said, letting out a snicker.

"*Not* funny," Tuyet said, sounding angry.

Hally hurried to change the subject. "What seems weirdest to me is why Mr. Crowhurst didn't let us try to put out the fire."

"'Cause he's a coward," Jason said. "And nothing's weirder than being locked in his stupid van. I'm gonna find a hammer and saw and get us out of here." He started crawling toward the tools, but Hally caught his ankle.

"If you bang up his van, we'll really be in trouble!" She held her other hand up to the light so that it cast a shadow on the wall of the van. Her hand shadow made a lop-eared rabbit. "I mean that," she said in a rabbity voice while she made her bunny wiggle its ears. "So calm down. Take two carrots and call me in the morning." Her shadow rabbit chewed an imaginary carrot.

"Oh, yeah?" Jason crawled back so he could get his hands into the ray of light. He cast a shadow that might have been a fat dog, or a lumpy camel. "Well, I don't like carrots. I'd rather eat an old rabbit. WOOOF!" His dog leaped at Hally's rabbit.

Hally squeaked and dropped her hand out of sight. She sat and laughed while Jason's dog, snorting and sniffing, searched the square of light.

"Where'd that rabbit go?" Jason growled, prowling his shadow back and forth.

"He went to call his friend, the moose," Tuyet giggled. She held up two hands, making a shape with a big rack of antlers. "Moose aren't afraid of dogs. They step on mean dogs' tails." She chased Jason's dog out of the light.

They played shadow games until they ran out of animals. Watching Tuyet make a dinosaur, Hally wondered how long they'd been locked in the van. A half hour? An hour? Quickly, before Jason could wonder the same thing, she asked him, "So who's the Viper, anyway?"

"The Viper? You never heard about the . . ." Jason's voice turned eerie. He gave an awful-sounding little cackle. "The *Viper?*"

"It's a snake?" she started to encourage him.

But Jason was already off and running. "There was this man. He got a phone call one day. He picks up the phone, 'Hello? Hello? Hello, is any-body there?' And this voice answers . . ." Jason's own voice turned into an evil growl. "It says, 'The Viper is coming in two months!' Click— it hangs up the phone.

"'Oh, gosh,' the man says, 'what's a viper? That's weird.' But after a few days, he forgets all about it. Until...a month later, sometime after midnight, the phone rings. And the same voice says, 'The Viper...is coming in...one month! Ha, ha, ha, ha, ha.'"

His laugh was so devilishly scary that Tuyet and Hally giggled along with him.

"So now he's getting worried," Jason continued. "'Who's this viper? What's he gonna do to me when he comes?' The man puts a new lock on the front door. He puts a big lock on the back door. Then he figures he's safe. But... two weeks later...late at night...the phone rings...and a voice says..." Jason's voice dropped to a hissing, unearthly whisper, "'The Viper is coming in TWO WEEKS!'

"So now the guy is *really* spooked. He goes out and buys a Doberman, even though he's allergic to dogs. But one week later, midnight, the phone rings again. And the voice says, 'Don't forget... the Viper is coming in ONE...WEEK.'"

Hally and Tuyet listened, spellbound, while

the Viper kept calling. He called to say he was coming in three days...two days...one day, and the poor man in Jason's story went crazy. He nailed his front door shut. He nailed his back door shut. He put bars on all the windows, and on the final day, he hid upstairs with the Doberman, shivering and shaking.

"And then he hears a bump on the outside wall...just below...the window," Jason whispered. "And then a shadow falls across the glass! The dog starts whining and puts its paws over its eyes. The man's shaking in his shoes. But he looks up, and this little old guy with white hair is standing on a ladder. He's holding a...hose. And a...sponge. And he says..." Jason's voice changed to a cheery, singsong voice with a silly accent, "'Hello, I'm the Vindow Viper! I've come to vipe your vindows!'"

"Oooh, that's awful!" Hally laughed. Jason was hooting so loudly at his own joke that he didn't hear her.

"The Viper...ha, *ha*, ha, *ha*," he chortled evilly.

"But you're not really going to send that Viper letter to Mom's boyfriend, Jason," Hally said, when she could breathe again.

"You can't," Tuyet agreed. "What if he doesn't know it's a joke?"

Jason stopped laughing. "I hope he doesn't," he said. "I hope the Hyena's so scared he nails himself shut inside his own house and never comes out again. I hope—" He let out a yelp as the back door to the van flew open.

Crowhurst stood in the van doorway. "Okay, you can come out now," he said.

Jason scrambled out first. "What took you so long?" he demanded, as the girls hopped down beside him. They were parked near the bingo hall on Broadway, Hally noticed.

Crowhurst scowled at him. "What do you mean, long? I've only been gone five minutes. I had to call the fire department. From a pay phone." He jerked his chin toward a pay phone across the street.

Hally stared at him. "Five minutes? You were gone a lot longer than that!"

Crowhurst bent down and stuck his mustache right in Hally's face. "No...I...wasn't!" he snarled. "And anybody who says I *was*..."

Hally would have backed up, but there was no place to go with the van behind her. So she gulped and glared back at him. She felt Jason bump into her as he moved to stand closer to her side. Tuyet touched her arm to warn her to be quiet.

But before Hally could think of what to say, a siren whooped in the distance. Crowhurst straightened and turned toward the sound. Another siren sounded from farther away. Then yet another wailed, and they could hear the roar of its engine as it raced for the fire.

"See?" he said, looking back at Hally and smirking. "What'd I tell you? I called 'em, and now they're going. And I've got to go, too. I said I'd meet 'em at the fire. So you kids get on home."

"Let's go," Tuyet said, and she grabbed Hally's arm.

But Hally was mad now. "Wait a minute!" she demanded, as Crowhurst turned away. "What about Tuyet? You owe her some money for painting."

Crowhurst turned back. He looked surprised, then he gave an ugly laugh. He pointed in the direction of the house, to a pink glow in the sky. "A lot of good her painting does me now. So beat it! I gotta get to that fire."

"Can you believe that?" Hally asked as they watched him drive away.

"Let's go watch his house burn to the ground," Jason said.

The rosy glow in the sky was even brighter now, and sirens seemed to be swarming from everywhere. Hally was tempted, but she shook her head. "I told Dad we'd be home by 10:00, and I bet it's past that by now."

"And who wants to see Mr. Crowhurst again?" Tuyet added. "Not me!"

So they walked back to Kerry Hill. By the time they got there, the glow of Crowhurst's burning house seemed to light up half the sky.

ACCUSED!

"You should have seen it!" Hally exclaimed, as Tuyet led them to the yard behind her house the next morning. "The whole inside of his house is burned out. You can look right through the wall into that first-floor apartment. It looks like the inside of a barbecue grill."

"Or a burned-up marshmallow," Jason chimed in. "Except everything's wet from the fire hoses. We missed a great fire," he added wistfully.

"I promised my aunt and uncle I would mow the lawn," Tuyet said, carefully pouring gasoline from a can into a mower. "Maybe we could take a walk over there after I'm done."

"Why not?" Hally said, just as the front door-bell rang. She and Jason tagged along as Tuyet ran into the house to answer it.

When Tuyet opened the front door, they saw Crowhurst and a police officer standing on the porch. Behind them stood a woman wearing the tan uniform of a Newport firefighter. "I'm Officer Swinburne," the police officer said. "This is Private Belli of the fire department's arson section." Officer Swinburne nodded toward Crowhurst. "And I believe you already know Mr. Crowhurst." He paused for a moment, then said, "May we come in?"

Tuyet's eyes looked very large. She nodded, then stood back to let them inside.

Standing in Tuyet's living room, the three visitors seemed very tall. "Are your aunt and uncle here?" Officer Swinburne asked.

"No," Tuyet said in a small voice. "They're working. They won't be home until tonight."

Crowhurst was smiling a nasty little smile

under his mustache. That smile worried Hally. "What's the problem, sir?" she said, looking at Officer Swinburne.

"These are the other two kids I told you about," Crowhurst broke in. He motioned toward Jason and Hally.

Private Belli spoke for the first time. "We found a pair of sneakers—what was left of them—on a footstool in front of a television set," she said, looking at Tuyet. "The fire started in that room. It looks as if someone was smoking a cigarette, and carelessly let it fall on the sofa. The sofa probably smoldered for a while, but once the curtains caught, everything went up in blazes."

"You know anything about that?" Officer Swinburne asked Tuyet.

"Sure she does," Crowhurst said. "It's as plain as the nose on your face. She was watching TV and smoking, instead of painting like I hired her to do. I told you she was a firebug."

"I am *not* a firebug!" Tuyet exclaimed. "And I do *not* smoke!"

"She almost burned down her own house last year, smoking cigarettes. And now she's burned down mine," Crowhurst sneered.

"That's not true!" Hally shouted. "How could Tuyet have been watching TV? That apartment was locked. We tried the door."

"You tried the door and you found it was open," Crowhurst insisted. "That apartment was vacant, so I left it unlocked. You and your brother were there, too, goofing off with Tuyet, weren't you? That's why you're lying now—to protect her and yourself."

"*You're* the liar!" Jason broke in. He marched right up to Crowhurst and gave him his fiercest scowl. He looked mad enough to kick the man's kneecap.

"That's enough," Officer Swinburne said and frowned at Crowhurst. "I'll handle this." He turned back to Tuyet. "I want to speak to your aunt and uncle," he told her. "And to your parents," he added, looking at Hally and Jason. "We need to get to the bottom of this. Bring them to the station, tomorrow night at 6:30. Do you understand?"

"Yes," Tuyet whispered.

Hally and Jason nodded.

Officer Swinburne and Private Belli didn't look happy at all. But Crowhurst was trying not to smirk as Tuyet showed them out. She shut the door, then burst into tears.

Hally ran to hug her. "Don't worry, Tuyet. It's going to be okay."

"Yeah," Jason said. He took a karate stance and slashed the air with his hands. "We'll fix that old werewolf. You wait and see."

A short while later, the three kids sat at the kitchen table. While Hally had helped Tuyet mow the lawn, Jason had made them peanut butter and banana sandwiches. A big smear of peanut butter on his cheek looked like a stripe of war paint. "It's simple," he said. "Crowhurst framed you."

"Framed?" Tuyet repeated. She picked up her sandwich, frowned at it, and put it down again.

"Yeah, he made it look like you set the place on fire." His last word sounded like "firomph," because Jason had taken a monstrous bite of sandwich, but Hally and Tuyet got the message.

"He's right," Hally said. "That's why he took your shoes, Tuyet. To make it look like you were sitting on that sofa. And it must have been him we heard—remember that sneeze? I bet he'd just started the fire—the smoke made him sneeze."

"And that's what I smelled!" Jason crowed. "I told you I had a bionic nose!"

"And that's why he gave us that leftover brown paint," Tuyet said slowly. "He didn't care what color we painted the walls. Because he knew the house was going to burn down."

"And that's why he gave you a radio and turned it up so loud," Hally added and jumped to her feet, she was so excited. "He didn't want you to hear him while he set the fire downstairs!"

"But why would he burn down his own house?" Tuyet wondered. "That makes no sense."

"I don't know why he'd do it," Hally said, "but I'm going to find out. He's not going to call any friend of mine a firebug!" She pulled Tuyet to her feet. "So let's go."

"Where?" mumbled Jason with his mouth full.

"To the scene of the crime. Maybe we'll find some clues." Hally put a finger on the tip of Jason's nose. "But first, wipe your face."

Standing in the yard in front of the burned-out house a short while later, Hally hoped her worry didn't show. It was easy to talk about finding clues. But any clues to Crowhurst's crime had gone up in smoke. How were they going to prove that they didn't start the fire?

"It's a wreck!" Tuyet whispered. "If they think I did this, will they put me in jail?"

"You didn't start this fire, and we're going to prove that," Hally said. She tucked her arm through Tuyet's. "Let's go look through the side windows. They were closest to the sofa."

The windows had no glass left in them. But peering through their charred frames, all Hally and her friends could see was a scorched and blackened wall.

"Hey!" a boy's voice called behind them. "Get away from there! That house isn't safe!"

Hally turned to see a boy about her age standing on the porch of the house next door. He had hair as black as Tuyet's, but his was curly. His nose was pug with lots of freckles.

"Yeah?" Jason bristled. "Says who?"

"Says my dad. He's the fire chief."

"What's his name?" Jason demanded, as if he knew each and every firefighter in town.

"Eddie. Eddie Machado, same as mine," the boy answered.

As he came down the steps, Hally put a hand

on Jason's shoulder. They didn't need anybody else mad at them. "Well, Eddie Machado," she asked with a smile, "were you home last night? Did you see the fire?"

Eddie looked embarrassed. "Only the last part," he admitted. "Dad and I were at bingo last night. So was Mr. Crowhurst—the owner of this house."

"No, he wasn't!" Jason sputtered. "He was here, burning his own house down."

"You're crazy!" Eddie said. "He couldn't have torched his own house. He was at bingo all night. Everybody saw him. Especially when he made a fool of himself." He told them the story. "He stood up and yelled bingo, and everybody thought he won. But when they checked his card, it turned out he was wrong. He'd put a marker on the wrong square. So he apologized, and then he left. I guess he felt silly."

"He said he was going to bingo," Hally recalled. "So I guess he did go there after he showed Tuyet what he wanted her to paint."

"But then he snuck back to set the fire," Jason added. "We heard him and smelled the smoke."

Eddie shook his head. "He stayed at bingo all night."

Hally got an idea. "Do you know what time he got there and what time he left?" she asked.

"Sure do," Eddie frowned, trying to recall. "I saw him come in at 7:30. I remember, because he walked over and asked my dad what time it was. He also asked my dad the time just before he left. It was 9:45."

"So he was at bingo from 7:30 until 9:45," Hally repeated.

"Right," Eddie agreed. "And then I guess he drove here, and rescued those dumb kids who started the fire. And then he called in the alarm. My dad was called out to the fire about fifteen minutes after Mr. Crowhurst left. But when the trucks got here, the house was up in flames."

"He set up an alibi," Hally said, thinking it

out. "He made sure a firefighter noticed him at 7:30. Then he made everybody notice him again when he yelled 'Bingo!' But sometime *between* 7:30 and 9:45, he snuck out of the hall. He came back here, set out Tuyet's shoes, lit a cigarette, and put it on the couch."

"Then he ran upstairs and grabbed us!" said Jason, following Hally's reasoning. "He locked us in the van, and went *back* to the bingo game—that's what he did!"

Tuyet nodded and kept on nodding. "That's why it seemed we were in the van a long time— because we were! He played bingo until he was sure his house was on fire. Then he left the hall at 9:45 and waited a few minutes more before he called in the alarm."

Eddie stared from one to the other of them. "You mean you're the kids Crowhurst rescued? Well, you guys are crazy! You must have breathed too much smoke," he said flatly.

"No, we're not crazy," Hally said. "I know

that's how he did it. The only thing I don't know is *why* Crowhurst would burn his own house down."

"That part's simple," Eddie offered. "People do that for the insurance money." He turned to look at the burned-out house. "And you know, he's been trying to sell that place for the last year with no luck. He sure wasn't going to get any money that way."

"You mean if his house is burned down, Crowhurst gets money?" Jason shook his head. "That's crazy."

"If his house is burned down *by accident,* they give him money," Eddie corrected. "If Crowhurst burned it down on purpose, they give him jail time."

"And so that's why he's blaming Tuyet," Hally said. She turned back to Eddie. "You know, we didn't set that fire. Crowhurst did. But we have to prove that to the police."

"How are you going to do that?" Eddie asked.

"I don't know," Hally admitted. "But I know one thing. You sure know a lot about fires, Eddie Machado. And we could sure use your help. How about it?"

The boy pursed his lips and made a tuneless little whistle. Then he grinned. "Sure, why not? My dad's job is tough enough, without people setting fires on purpose. Besides, I never liked old Crowhurst anyway. Where do we start?"

CHAPTER 7

SEARCHING FOR CLUES

Sitting on the steps that led to the Machados' front porch, Hally, Jason, and Tuyet told Eddie about the fire.

"So that's why he put up the curtains!" Eddie exclaimed, when they got to that part of the story. "Crowhurst hung those curtains yesterday, in the apartment where the fire started. I saw him through the window."

"Was there anything on those windows before?" Hally asked eagerly.

"Sure, he took down some perfectly good blinds," Eddie said.

"But blinds wouldn't burn as easily as cloth

curtains," Tuyet observed. "He thought of everything."

"He must have missed something," Jason said. "We just have to find it."

"Aha!" Hally cried and jumped to her feet. "I know!" She shot her fist into the air and stamped a little victory dance while the others stared at her. She danced up to Tuyet and tweaked her hair. "Does Crowhurst smoke, Tuyet?"

Tuyet wrinkled her nose, thought, and shook her head. "I don't think I've ever seen him with a cigarette."

"Neither have I," Eddie agreed. "So?"

"So where did he get a cigarette to start the fire?" Hally asked.

"He bought it . . . ," Jason said slowly. "And maybe, if we're lucky, he bought it around here." He jumped to his feet, and did a few shuffling steps of the Iowa Glide Stride. "And maybe, if we're very, *very* lucky, somebody will remember him buying cigarettes!"

"All *right!*" Eddie yelled. He leaped down three steps to land beside Jason, and gave him a low five. "Great idea, Hally! Let's check out the stores."

For a small town, Newport had a lot of places to buy cigarettes, the friends soon learned. They started at the corner store nearest Mr. Crowhurst's house. "A grumpy guy with a bushy mustache?" the clerk said. "Lives down the street? Sure I know him. But I've never sold him cigarettes. Don't think he even smokes."

The story was the same at every store. No one remembered selling cigarettes to a man with a mustache. Or if they did, then the mustache was red. Or the mustache was attached to the face of Mr. Kerr, the yacht captain, or Mr. Gaines, the carpenter.

"Well, it was a good idea," Tuyet sighed, as they trudged out of a drugstore on Bellevue Avenue. "But maybe he bought the cigarettes out of town. Or borrowed some from a friend."

"Or somebody just forgot his ugly face," Jason grumbled.

"My feet hurt," Eddie added.

"We can't give up," Hally said. "We need this clue. Aren't there any more stores in town, Eddie?"

There was one, but it was a long walk down the hill and then along the waterfront to the south end of town. Eddie was not the only one with sore feet by the time they limped to its door.

A very large dog, with a soft golden coat and sad brown eyes, sprawled in the doorway. Jason stopped to pat him. The others stepped over the dog and entered the store.

A bored-looking young man chewed gum as he waited behind the cash register. Hally gave him a hopeful smile. "I wonder if you could tell me," she said politely, "if a man with a big black mustache bought some cigarettes here yesterday? Or maybe the day before?"

"Couldn't tell you," the young man said. He

blew a wet, pink bubble and let it pop. "I don't pay attention to mustaches."

Hally felt her last hope fade, and beside her, Tuyet's shoulders sagged. "You're sure you can't remember? A grouchy-looking man? His mustache droops?"

The young man shrugged. "Sorry."

"Oh, come on, Ray," said a voice across the room. Hally turned to find a skinny boy with sun-bleached yellow hair standing by the comic book rack. He'd been reading a Spiderman comic, and now he put it away. "I was in here when he bought them, remember? The guy who didn't care what brand you gave him, as long as it was the cheapest?"

"Oh, yeah," said the clerk.

"That's him!" cried Hally, as she hurried over to the boy. She felt like hugging him.

He had blue eyes, round wire-rimmed glasses, and was a bit taller than Eddie. "Why do you want to know?" he asked her.

92

"Well, that's a long story," she said. "But tell me, would you know this man again if you saw him?" She held her breath.

"Sure I would. I know practically everybody in Newport, including your friend here," the boy said, exchanging a grin with Eddie. "The guy who bought the cigarettes was Mr. Crowhurst. He lives over on Kerry Hill." When Hally and Tuyet shrieked with delight, he added, "Now will you tell me the story?"

"Sure thing!" Hally said, then she glanced around the store. "Hey, where's my brother? Didn't he come in with us?"

Jason was outside, sound asleep, his head resting on the big, shaggy dog. "This is Sam," the boy said, patting the dog. "He's a golden retriever, and I'm a Kerry. Joe Kerry."

"Was Kerry Hill named after your family?" Tuyet asked him.

Joe laughed. "Kerry Hill's called that 'cause it used to be full of Irish. Supposedly, they all came from County Kerry in Ireland. Now what's your story?"

Once he'd heard it, Joe let out a long whistle. "The guy's a real rat, isn't he?"

"Yes, he is," Hally said, as the others nodded in agreement. "But now that we have you as a witness..."

"I'll be glad to help," Joe said. "But that won't be enough to convince the cops. If Crowhurst can prove he was at bingo from 7:30 to 9:45, then he couldn't have set the fire."

"You're right," Hally admitted gloomily. "We need someone who saw him sneak out of the hall, between those two times." She turned to Eddie. "Eddie, think real hard. Who was at bingo?"

Eddie scratched his head. "Umm, old Mr. Costello. Sister Rachel Marie." He tugged on an ear. "Mrs. Ames..."

"Mrs. Ames!" Hally laughed. "She was there? Why, she and her husband own the house we live in, and they live downstairs from us. Let's go ask her."

They didn't have to walk far on their sore feet before Joe found them a ride. As a battered old pickup truck drove past them, he grinned and stuck out his thumb.

The driver was a cousin of Joe's, a lobsterman on his way home from his boat. Hally and her friends climbed into the back of his pickup.

Sam liked the ride as much as the kids. Standing up in back, he stuck his nose around the cab and snorted noisily, and whacked everybody with his tail, but otherwise his manners were fine. Jason was the one who got into trouble.

No one noticed when he discovered the ice chest beside them was full of lobsters. But they all noticed when he stuck a live lobster down the back of Eddie's T-shirt.

When Eddie screamed, their driver nearly rammed a car that was stopped at a stop sign in front of them. He was almost as mad as

Eddie, who had turned cherry red by the time they got the lobster out of his shirt.

Hally couldn't let Eddie hang Jason out the back of the truck by his heels like he wanted to. But with Eddie and Joe's help, she held Jason down for the rest of the ride and let Sam lick his face until he shrieked for mercy. By the time they reached Kerry Hill, Eddie had cheered up again, and Jason was cleaner than he'd been in hours.

"I washed my face to come visit you," he told Mrs. Ames.

While the other kids rolled their eyes, Mrs. Ames looked up from the toaster she had taken apart, and patted him on the back. "That's a good boy," she chuckled and gave him a cookie. He smirked at Hally behind her back.

Mrs. Ames gave the others cookies as well, then she gave them something even better. "That old Crowhurst?" she said when Hally asked. "He sat right across from me at bingo.

Borrowed a dollar from me and never even said thank you. I was glad when he wandered off."

"Where did he go?" Hally asked, and beside her, Tuyet crossed her fingers.

"Said he was going to the bathroom," Mrs. Ames said. "But that was the last I saw of him. Until he claimed he won the bingo, about an hour later."

"So...Eddie says Crowhurst yelled bingo at about 9:35," Hally figured. "And he left his place at your table at about 8:30—would that be about right, Mrs. Ames?"

"That's right," she nodded.

"But that doesn't prove that he left the hall, went back to his house, set the fire, and then pretended to rescue you guys," Joe pointed out, once they'd left Mrs. Ames.

"What we need is some way to prove that Mr. Crowhurst came back to his house," Tuyet agreed. "Or they'll keep blaming me for the fire."

Hally touched her arm. "They won't blame

you, Tuyet. We won't let them. We've got until tomorrow night to find that proof, and we're going to do it."

But she didn't have a clue what that proof might be—or how they'd find it.

CHAPTER 8

THE KERRY HILL
CASECRACKERS

The next day was gray and gloomy. It rained so hard in the morning that Hally wondered if Newport Harbor would rise up and flood the town.

The night before, she had told her father about Crowhurst and his accusation. "I'm going to have a talk with that guy!" Jim Watkins fumed. But he hadn't been able to find Crowhurst, not last night, and not again this morning. Finally, he had gone off scowling to his job at the Newport Sailing Club. "But I'll be there with you at the station tonight," he promised before he left.

"Still, we need some way to prove that Crowhurst left the bingo hall," Hally worried aloud.

Jason looked up from his Viper letter, which he had pulled out when their father left the house. "Mrs. Ames is going to tell the police what she knows," he reminded her. He pasted down one last piece of newspaper, and his message read: "THE VIPER IS COMING IN 2 MONTHS!"

"But then Crowhurst will just claim that he moved to another part of the hall." Hally paced back and forth. Outside the window, the rain had stopped, and the sun was peeking through the clouds. "You're not really going to send that to Mom's boyfriend," she added.

"Just watch me," Jason growled. Carefully, he folded the letter, stuck it in an envelope, and addressed it to "Mr. Hyena Abrams."

Hally shook her head. She ought to stop him, she knew, but they hadn't had a real fight yet, and she didn't want to start one over something as silly as a Viper letter. Returning to the window, she saw Tuyet turn the corner. Her friend looked very small and unhappy. She didn't walk around the puddles in front of her; she trudged straight through them.

"We've still got till 6:30 tonight to find our proof," Hally reminded her when she walked through the back door.

But Tuyet did not look comforted. "Yes," she said quietly.

They didn't find much to smile at that day. After the rain stopped, Joe arrived on his bike, with Sam bounding beside him. Eddie joined them soon after that. But nobody had any good ideas.

They spent all afternoon looking for other people who had been in the bingo hall with Crowhurst. But most of those people were not at home. "Guess he's at work, too," Eddie said, looking up at a closed front door, as he rubbed his knuckles, which were sore from knocking.

"Oh, we're hurtin' for certain," Jason sang. He strolled over to a nearby mailbox. Before Hally knew what he was up to, he had dropped the Viper letter down its slot. "Hurtin' for certain," he sang again and returned her glare with a "fooled you!" smirk.

"We'll be hurtin' for certain, if we can't find some proof," Eddie grumbled. "Let's see, Sister Rachel lives behind the church... She's the last one I can remember seeing there. Maybe she saw something."

But Sister Rachel Marie had gone to visit a sick friend.

"She was our last hope," Eddie admitted.

"And it's getting late," Joe added, as across town, the bell in the Trinity Church steeple chimed 6:00. "I guess we better go to the police station. We don't want to be late."

"Oh, we're hurtin' for certain," Jason sang under his breath.

"*You* will be hurtin' for certain if you don't

quit singing that," Hally threatened him. They were all discouraged enough as it was.

"That's what Jason was dancing to when Crowhurst ran upstairs and yelled 'Fire!'" Tuyet explained to Joe.

"He was?" Joe stopped so suddenly that Eddie bumped into his back. "On the radio?" He grabbed Hally's sleeve. "What station?"

She squinted, trying to remember. "One hundred three FM?"

"All *right!*" Joe punched his fist skyward. "My uncle's best friend is a DJ on that station!"

"So?" Hally said.

"So I've got to talk to him!" Joe tore off down the hill.

"Wait, Joe! You're our best witness!" Hally yelled after him.

He stopped, turned, and yelled back, "I'll see you at the police station!"

"If he doesn't show up, we're cooked," Eddie muttered.

"We'll be hurt—" Hally, Tuyet, and Eddie turned to glare, and Jason stopped singing in mid-note.

At the police station, everyone was waiting for them. Tuyet's aunt and uncle looked worried; Hally's father looked mad. Mrs. Ames gave Hally a slight smile and wave. Crowhurst wore a nasty little smirk whenever Hally looked his way. Eddie's father, wearing his fire chief uniform, Private Belli, Officer Swinburne, and Police Chief Mancuso weren't smiling at anyone.

"Mr. Crowhurst has made a very serious charge," the police chief said when everyone was seated in a back room. "Let's hear his story first."

Hally could barely sit still while Crowhurst told how he had hired Tuyet to paint his house. How he had warned Hally and her "bratty" brother off his property. He explained how he had played bingo all evening.

"You saw me there, Ed," he said, nodding

at Eddie's father. "Well, I left the hall at 9:45. Drove over to my house, maybe 9:50, and smelled smoke. The first-floor apartment was burning like a bonfire! I ran upstairs, and these fool kids were dancing to the radio instead of painting. I guess they'd been goofing off all evening—watching TV, smoking cigarettes, having themselves a great time. Anyway, I hustled 'em out of there. I threw 'em in my van, drove to the nearest phone, and called the fire department."

He shrugged. "That's about it. She—" He jerked his head in Tuyet's direction. "She and her little...friends burned my house down."

Before anyone could stop him, Jason stood up on his chair. "That's a lie from start to finish, and I bet you choke on your mustache for telling it!"

"That's enough, young man!" the police chief snapped. Jim Watkins scooped Jason off his chair, then sat him down again with a warning shake.

Hally held up her hand. "Chief Mancuso?

You've heard Mr. Crowhurst's story. Now can Tuyet and I tell you ours?"

For a second, it looked as if the police chief might say no. Then he nodded stiffly. Hally and Tuyet walked to the front of the room. Hally's legs were shaking, and beside her, Tuyet trembled like a young tree in a storm. Hally stared past the adults. Where was Joe when they needed him?

"The story starts last year," Hally said in a shaky voice. "Two things happened. First, one of Mr. Crowhurst's rental houses burned down. And I bet he was paid insurance money for that house. Is that right?" She looked directly at Mr. Crowhurst.

The man stirred, looked surprised that she was talking to him, then nodded. "Yeah, so what?" he said.

"So if you lost another house this year, the police might think that was pretty strange unless—"

Mr. Crowhurst lurched to his feet with a roar. "Are you accusing me of—"

"Sit!" the police chief commanded. Crowhurst sat.

"The police and other people would wonder, unless the second fire had a pretty clear reason for happening," Hally continued. "So he found somebody to blame it on. And he chose Tuyet." She smiled at her friend and turned the story over to her.

In a whisper so tiny that everyone had to lean forward in their chairs to hear, Tuyet told them about her experiment with cigarettes last year. The accidental fire in her bedroom. And how Crowhurst had been calling her a firebug ever since.

"So he asked Tuyet to come paint his apartment," Hally went on. "But first, he did a few things that morning."

Eddie stood up. "He hung some new curtains in the empty apartment downstairs! Took down some perfectly good blinds, then hung these long cloth curtains in their place."

"And he did something else that was pretty strange," Hally added. "But our witness for that isn't here yet."

She went on to tell about Crowhurst's strange actions—the ugly gray and brown paint he gave them to paint onto white walls that didn't need painting. She told about Crowhurst turning the radio up loud. When she said that he left with Tuyet's shoes, everyone looked at him. Crowhurst sat there, shaking his head from side to side.

"And when he left his house he went to bingo," Hally said. "And the first thing he did when he got there was..." She nodded at Eddie.

Eddie whispered in his father's ear, then Mr. Machado stood. "He asked me what time it was, and I told him it was 7:30."

"Then he sat near Mrs. Ames to play bingo," Hally said.

"But he left about 8:30!" Mrs. Ames cried out. "Said he was going to the bathroom, but I didn't see him again for a *long* time."

"Big deal!" Crowhurst growled. "I don't know why we're listening to this nonsense! I simply sat someplace else."

"No," Hally said. "You slipped out of the hall and went back to your house. You snuck into the first-floor apartment and made it look as if Tuyet had been watching TV. You lit a cigarette and put it on the sofa. Then you pulled the drapes onto the sofa so they would catch fire easily."

Then she told how they had smelled the smoke upstairs and gone down to investigate. She told of the sneeze behind the locked door. "We went back upstairs, and a few minutes later, Mr. Crowhurst showed up. He yelled that there was a fire. When he got us downstairs, we saw it had just started. But he wouldn't try to put it out." Police Chief Mancuso and Eddie's father exchanged glances, then looked at Crowhurst suspiciously.

Crowhurst squirmed in his seat for an instant, then leaped to his feet, nearly knocking his chair over. "I've heard enough of this!" he blustered, glaring at the police chief. "Mancuso, I don't know why you bother to listen to this . . . this . . . " He jabbed a finger at Hally, "this mouthy brat and her lying, foreign, firebug friend. I do know this, though. I don't have to stay here and listen to lies from a bunch of kids!"

He started for the door, but Chief Mancuso stepped in front of him. "I told you once to sit," he said quietly. "I won't tell you again."

Crowhurst went sputtering and muttering back to his chair.

"And Hally's not a mouthy brat!" Jason yelled at him. "She might be mouthy, but she's not a—" Mr. Watkins put his hand on Jason's shoulder and leaned to say something in his ear. Jason shut his mouth.

Chief Mancuso gave him a long, hard stare. Then he cleared his throat and turned back to Hally. "Why don't you continue, young lady?" he said.

Hally gave Jason a hurried smile. Then she told everyone how Crowhurst had locked them in his van and gone away for a long time. "To make his alibi, he went back to the hall. He played another game, and then yelled bingo. But he hadn't really won."

"That's right!" Mrs. Ames and Eddie's father called out together.

"He just wanted everybody to notice he was there," Hally said. "Then to make sure of that, he asked Mr. Machado the time again, and it was 9:45. So he left the hall. By then he knew his house must be on fire. So he called the fire department, and then he let us out of the van." Hally took a deep breath. "That's what really happened."

"That's the stupidest thing I ever heard!"

Crowhurst yelled. "There's no way to prove that!"

The police chief nodded. "It's a nice theory, young lady, but I don't think I could build a case on it."

Just then, Joe Kerry and a bearded young man burst through the door.

"But here's our proof!" Hally cried. "Joe, tell them what you saw at the store."

Joe pointed at Crowhurst. "He bought a pack of cigarettes. But he didn't know what brand to buy, because he doesn't smoke. He just asked for whatever was cheapest. Ray Cottrell's the clerk. You can check it out with him."

Eddie's father let out a long, low whistle. Crowhurst jumped to his feet. "That doesn't prove anything!" he cried hoarsely. "I bought those for a friend!"

"I'll want the name of the friend," the police chief said.

"Uhhh..." Crowhurst stood there, opening

and closing his mouth like a fish out of water.

Meanwhile, Joe whispered to Tuyet and Hally.

"And I have two final questions," Hally said when Joe was done. "First, what time did you say it was when you—ah—rescued us, Mr. Crowhurst?"

He chewed on his mustache. "Let's see... uhh...err...I called in the alarm at about 10:00. So it would have been just before that. About 9:55."

"And you say we were *dancing* when you ran into the room?" Hally added a note of disbelief to her voice.

"You're darn right you were dancing!" Crowhurst pointed at Jason. "That mouthy little midget was dancing to a song called 'Hurtin' for Certain!' If I hadn't rescued him, he'd *really* have been hurting, but look at all the thanks I get!"

Joe's bearded friend stepped forward. He carried a big book, which he now opened.

"I'm John Kelly, disc jockey for station WFSH, Newport," he announced, then looked down at his logbook. "And Mr. Crowhurst is absolutely correct. Two nights ago I did play a song called 'Hurtin' for Certain.'" He looked up and fixed his eyes on Crowhurst. "It played at precisely . . . 9:00."

"Well, well, well," said Eddie's father. "Looks like we have an arsonist on our hands." Crowhurst's ears turned bright red and his shoulders slumped.

Chief Mancuso stood. He walked over to Hally and Tuyet and shook their hands. "Kids," he said solemnly, "that was some pretty fancy detective work. You and your pals just cracked the case." He smiled. "You're all free to leave now. Looks like the one we need to have a chat with is Mr. Crowhurst."

He might have said something more, but Hally and her friends were cheering too loud to hear him.

While the others lingered inside the police station, Hally and her friends gathered outside on the front steps. Sam was waiting for them there. He barked and wagged his tail while Hally and Tuyet hugged each other.

Eddie and Joe traded high fives, then they both socked Jason on the shoulders. He yelped, but he looked very pleased—at least he did until Sam gave him a big, sloppy kiss on the nose.

"Gee," Eddie gloated, "we're so good at mysteries, we ought to go into the business. We could be detectives!"

"We're casecrackers," Joe agreed.

"That's us," Hally laughed. "The Kerry Hill Casecrackers!"

"I know another mystery we could try to . . . to crack," Tuyet said. "My uncle Chau-Li says that a ghost is living out in the old lighthouse at Hazard Island. He saw it himself, from his fishing boat!"

"I don't believe in ghosts," Joe sniffed.

"Well, if it isn't a ghost, then what is it?" Tuyet challenged him.

"I guess that's a question the Kerry Hill Casecrackers will have to answer," Hally said.

"And the other question is, what's the Hyena going to think of the letter I sent him?" Jason added, then gave his best Viper cackle. He started down the stairs with Sam tagging at his heels.

Hally groaned and rolled her eyes at her friends. "Guess I better go keep him out of trouble."

"Wait for us!" Tuyet called as she, Joe, and Eddie clattered down the steps after Hally.

Up the street, in the gathering darkness, Sam barked as Jason hollered something back at him. The Kerry Hill Casecrackers laughed and broke into a run.

THE KeRRy HILL CASECRACKERS

*Join the Kerry Hill Casecrackers
for each one of these adventures:*

#1 The Case of the Furtive Firebug

#2 The Case of the Lighthouse Ghost

#3 The Case of the Squeaky Thief

#4 The Case of the Mysterious Codes

ABOUT THE AUTHORS

The authors of The Kerry Hill Casecrackers are Peggy Nicholson and John F. Warner. A native Texan, a graduate of Brown University, and a former high school art teacher, Nicholson has been writing and living in Newport for the past several years. The author of several Harlequin novels, she was twice a finalist for the Golden Medallion, awarded for the best romance novel of the year. She has also published plays and short stories in textbook anthologies and has written several books for young readers.

A former teacher, editor, and publishing executive, Warner is the founder of a Newport business that creates and produces educational materials and children's books. He is also the author of more than 70 short stories, plays, and nonfiction pieces that appear in a variety of anthologies. He has written hundreds of magazine and newspaper articles, as well as several books for Lerner Publications Company.